My Princess

by Billy Aronson

Years ago, I was very lonely.

I lived with hundreds of uncles, aunts, brothers, sisters, and cousins. There were lots of frogs to play with.

So, why did I feel lonely? Because there was someone special I wanted to get to know. Someone who didn't even know I was alive.

I wanted to be friends with this special someone. But it wasn't going to be easy. She was *very* different from me. She was a human being.

From the first time I saw this girl I liked her. I don't know why! Maybe it was her curly hair. Maybe it was her crooked smile.

Every afternoon she walked right by the pond. But she never even noticed me.

I really wanted to be her friend. I just didn't know how to tell her!

I tried telling her in the morning. I tried telling her at lunch time. I tried telling her in the afternoon. I tried telling her in the evening. But she just didn't understand.

Being understood by a human being can be hard!

Having lots of uncles and aunts is great. When you have a problem, one of them always has an answer.

"Bring her a big, fat fly!" said Aunt Ribbit.

"Paint her a mud picture!" cried Uncle Bugs.

"No, no! Sing her a song!" insisted Uncle Croaker.

Uncle Croaker's idea interested me. My whole family loved to sing. On Friday nights we used to give free concerts.

We also loved telling stories. ("Little Green Riding Hood" and "Sleeping Froggy" were my favorites.)

Maybe I could show this girl how much I liked her by writing. . .

AN OPERA!

I decided to set a story to music to make an opera. That would show the girl that I wanted to be her friend.

First I wrote the music. Then I wrote the story. It was about a human princess who was locked in a castle by some ugly toads. One day a frog prince saw the princess. He wanted to be her friend. But the ugly toads told him to get lost. Of course the frog prince had to be clever to set the princess free.

I named it "The Human Princess."

There's another great thing about having lots of aunts and uncles. You always have plenty of actors to audition for parts. I only needed three toads. But my uncles and aunts were *very* good at making ugly faces! So I used all of them.

Aunt Ribbit batted her eyes. Uncle Croaker stuck his tongue out about three feet. Uncle Giggit wrapped his eyelids back around his head. Aunt Ribba–Dibbit swallowed her legs.

Some of my cousins wanted to be in the opera, too. So I let them be the prince's helpers. (All they had to do was follow the prince around and sing "Good idea!" once in a while.)

I would play the prince, of course. But who would be the princess?

Finding someone to play the "Human Princess" was hard. I needed someone with just the right look. None of my relatives looked the least bit human!

So I did something I'd never done before. I hopped over to the next pond.

At first I was worried. The frogs in the other pond looked just as froggy as my own relatives—maybe even froggier!

But then I found her.

She had lime green skin and a wide, rubbery smile. Her eyes were what I noticed first. They were different from other frogs' eyes. They were smaller. They didn't stick out quite as far. They were a little closer together. This girl frog looked just a little bit human.

I'd found just the right frog to play the "Human Princess"!

Her name was Bibbit. She was a little shy, but she agreed to help me out.

Now all the roles were filled, and we got right to work.

Bibbit had a beautiful singing voice! She quickly learned the songs.

A team of volunteers made scenery. The actors learned their lines. We rehearsed and rehearsed.

Finally, we were ready. It was show time!

The next time the human girl came to the pond,
we all hopped to our places. This was my big chance!

Luckily, the others didn't seem nervous. The toads
were great. Boy, were they ugly!

But I was so scared. As the show began I could
feel my legs tremble. I was sure I'd sing a wrong
note, or fall off a lily pad. What if the girl didn't look
at me? What if she just walked away?

I opened my mouth for my first song, but only a
squeak came out.

Just then, I felt a little tug on my shoulder. It was Bibbit. She was smiling. She gave me courage.

I took a deep breath and I began to sing. I was incredible! I sang with power. I leaped with grace. The other frogs could hardly believe it.

They weren't the only ones who noticed. There by the side of the pond, my new human friend was looking right at me— and smiling.

When the show was over, she clapped. I loved the applause. But did she know that I did it all for her? Did she understand that I wanted to be her friend?

I hopped out of the pond, right up to the girl's foot. Then I made a deep bow.

The girl didn't run away. She didn't budge. Instead, she reached down and petted my back!

She *had* understood. She wanted to be my friend, too.

"I'm happy for you," said Bibbit. Bibbit was one great friend.

Now the girl comes to the pond quite often. Sometimes I tell frog jokes. Sometimes, Bibbit and I sing frog songs together.

Bibbit and I have fun singing, hopping, playing, and swimming together.

I don't have much time for humans these days. (Bibbit and I have a few hundred tadpoles of our own to look after.) The girl is still my friend, but it's Bibbit who really matters.

Isn't it funny how things work out? The heroine of my opera turned out to be the heroine of my life!